SEVERANCE

A Fairy Tale Collection Novella

Inspired by Hans Christian Andersen's *The Little Mermaid*

M A Smith

Published by Fantasia Divinity © 2018

ISBN-13: 978-1987561340
ISBN-10: 1987561341

Published in the United States of America

First Publication: 2018

Published by Fantasia Divinity

Edited by: Amber M. Simpson

Cover © Germancreative, 2018

Fantasia Divinity Magazine
www.fantasiadivinitymagazine.com

Editor-in-Chief: Madeline L. Stout

Table of Contents

Fantasia Divinity's
Fairy Tale Collection:

Ravenous by Cassandra Schoeber
The Nightingale by JM Willaims - April 25, 2018
The Eighth Dwarf by R.A. Goli - June 15th, 2018
Cinderella's Kiss by Chris Brock - July 15th, 2018
The Charming Prince by David W. Landrum - Fall 2018
Nightwood by Elana Gomel - Early 2019
Eternity by Cindar Harrell - Summer 2019

SEVERANCE

Presented by Fantasia Divinity

For Stuart and Eleanor, with love

Severance

Chapter 1

I used to wonder if we belonged here, down among the wrecks and shoals and sunken things of the deep. Grandmother told me stories sometimes, when she thought Father did not hear, of a time when people walked with legs on land, under an unblemished sun, breathing in un-poisoned air. I sometimes thought she was spinning whimsies from thin water. But the way she told it...I half believed her.

Grandmother said (in whispers, when the last of the day's light shimmered on the sands of the seafloor) that thousands of years ago, we all had legs and feet, and breathed through the now redundant buttons of our noses. It was a strange concept. She said the ancient survivors of the Ravage took to the swamps and the shallows to survive and, over thousands of years, developed back into the fish-like creatures from which they had so long ago sprung. When she spied my father coming, gliding down the castle corridors in a murky mood, she hushed up. She was not afraid of him – Grandmother was afraid of nothing – but she did not want to bring trouble down on my head (for I was her favourite) with talk of this lost breed: Father had no time for such tales. He believed such speculation to be dangerous, and would not tolerate it.

Today his displeasure spins around him like eel agitated shale. "Audience chamber, if you please," he addresses me as he passes, a tepid current stirring the long strands of my silver-violet hair in his wake.

"You will do well to set an example," says Grandmother, managing to call after him without raising her voice.

My father turns, a hint of deferentiality in the set of his shoulders, the turn of his waist.

"Mother," he says, inclining his head slightly.

She takes this as her cue and whisks up and away in a sedate flurry of caudal fin and keel. The twelve oyster shells strung on her tail glow weakly in the diminishing light.

I watch her go, disappearing into the shade and shimmer of the tower, and when I turn back to accompany my father to the audience chamber, he is already out of sight.

I should hurry, but I do not. Instead, I slowly bob and weave my way along the passageway, letting my fingers brush the bright anemones that festoon the walls, feeling the delicate pulse and thrust of their little lives, relishing the almost imperceptible suck of each tentacle on my skin.

Two of my sisters, outside the audience chamber, watch my approach with cool disinterest. They must be relieved to be spared this particular ordeal, but they refuse to show it. You would not guess, from their small smiles and high held chins, how they had had to be dragged into this audience chamber by their hair to co-preside when, five moon turns since, there had been bloodshed over salvage at the border. They have not the stomachs for difficult decisions. Or guilt. That same hair, lately held tight in Father's fists, twines and separates around them, folds of black and skeins of yellow merging and pulling apart in the drifting current. A diffuse shaft of distant sunlight catches a curve of the wall's polished coral as I pass them, striking reflections from the scales of our tails, so that the waters are stabbed with brief and wavering glints of gold, grey and copper. One of the guards flanking the great stone door opens it at my approach. Inside, the water is tumultuous with the movement of bodies as courtiers and spectators jostle for position, attempting to get a better view of the man on trial.

My father, from his high seat, raises his hand for quiet, and the crowd hushes as I slip into my place beside him. How I hate this. The man, soon to be condemned, seeks my eyes, looking for mercy, but I cannot meet them. He is chained at the wrists, and I notice that his adipose fin is torn and bleeding.

"Father," I whisper. "This man is injured."

"He resisted being brought before me," my father replies shortly.

The proceedings begin. The case against the chained man is read out by the notary. It is suggested that Farner has been to the landmass beyond the eastern drift, well beyond the borders of the realm, risking radiation exposure and the subsequent contamination of our community. It is the contention of the court that Farner spent some small time on land, prone and gasping on the rocks, for reasons unclear. To everyone else, at least. Having been held in isolation for the turn of two hundred and forty tides, he has been judged clean and fit for trial.

The case proceeds. There are witnesses that swear they saw the man swim beyond the eastern drift. There is a 'friend' that remembers Farner speaking his desire to visit the landmass twenty-four tides before his disappearance. Farner's brother testifies to his sibling's courageous character, which only serves to strengthen the prosecution's case. There are a number of questions posed to the accused: they are all variations on 'why?'

Farner does not look at me again during the trial. He keeps his eyes downcast, and it is unbearable. He also refuses to answer any of the questions, merely shaking his head.

Finally, my father has heard enough, and raises himself up. The audience jostles and buzzes, but Farner is silent, eyes still held fast on the slowly shifting sand beneath us.

"You have transgressed our law," says Father. There is no emotion in his voice, but it is as implacable as the strata deep beneath us. If stone could speak, it would sound so. "It is my belief and my ruling that you went beyond the eastern clean cordon to satisfy a selfish curiosity that could have brought disease and corruption to our people. Knowing the risk you took in so doing, you must now prepare yourself to bear its consequences. You are banished from the realm, to fend for yourself forever beyond the cordons. This is my judgement."

The few quickly hushed voices of dismay are swallowed by the low pulse of approval that emanates from the assembled Folk like a heartbeat.

Father, lowering himself, looks to me, and the eyes of the assembled crowd also shift. It is my role to support my father's verdict, our custom that I parrot back his decree before it is carried out.

I remain seated. If Farner looks at me, in this instant, I do not like to think what will happen. But he doesn't, and so, lifting my chin, I simply say, "The judgement is banishment. Let it be done. In the name of the folk, I uphold this."

***

When it is all over, just before the last of the light fades, fracturing in bands of gold and green, I go to my room where I collect a small bag, woven from byssus. I take this with me to my private garden, which nestles against the Keep just as the clams from which the byssus is harvested cleave to the rock. I look around, ensuring my solitude. Happy that I am alone, I pull open the bag. Inside is a bright red flower, gaudy and beautiful; I gently bring it into the open, and it ululates with the movement of the water. It is hypnotic. I have never seen such a thing. Tendrils snake from its stem; I think of Grandmother's stories, and the word 'roots' comes into my mind. Hearing chatter from the castle behind me, I quickly dig a small hole in the pebbly sand of my garden, place the bottom section of the flower in the hole, and scrape the shale into a mound around its stem. It strives airwards, pulling against its captivity. It doesn't belong here.

I wish, then, that I had been brave enough to tell Father that Farner had risked his life to bring me back a flower.

Chapter 2

Farner had only been gone but five tides' turns when the shadow passed over the southern borders. Its belly slouched above the cordons, a bulging darkness that dispersed the pig-krill and the milnesiums, and stirred the kelp fields. My youngest sister told me this. She was there when it happened, at the nets, with a guard. Which is not where she should have been, or who she should have been with. She said they had watched the great shadow approach, a bulging cumulus that churned through the upper waters and ploughed light behind it in a fractured wake.

She was dispatched home immediately, of course, and the first I knew of these events was when, trailing agitated spume, she erupted into the garden of the Coral Keep and caught me up by the shoulders. I could feel the beat of her pulse through my skin, and I took her hands in my own.

"Amonie! What has happened?"

"Grandmother says it is a boat! It crossed at the southern border! It is approaching the Nest now, and moving yet. Father has sent the Sirens…"

It was enough. I dropped my sister's hands and hurtled from the Keep. The sea bed was silent, as the folk huddled for shelter in cave and chasm. The bivalve filter station stood abandoned, and the half-ploughed mangrove fields were left unsecured, tethers loose and weaving in the soft midday currents. At the edge of the commune, Grandmother floated alone, between sea bed and surface. The light from sky-wards glittered in shards on her dorsal and pelvic fins, and she shot out a hand as I passed her, pulling me back against the force of my own wake with a surprising strength. She looked at me, hard. And I looked back.

Finally, she spoke. "You must not help them. You cannot."

"I do not think the Sirens will be in need of my services, Grandmother." I tried, gently, to pull away. I could sense the commotion, not far distant.

"I do not mean the Sirens." She held my gaze a moment longer, and then dropped my arm. But I felt her eyes on my back as I sped through the waters.

I reached the Nest, winded and bright with fear and excitement. Father, surrounded by the seven Sirens, saw me instantly and glared in my direction, but did not break off to banish me back to the Keep. A few moments later, the Sirens rose upwards through the mellow waters of the deep, ascending beyond the indigos and turquoises as they neared the shadow of the boat which floated, still and silent, above us. Father sank back through the waters to join me, looking up past the layers of drift and current.

"Why are you here? You should be safe in the Keep."

"I wanted to see."

"You wanted to see." There was such bitterness in his voice that I cringed away from him.

But before I could retort, the Sirens, wavering high in the shallows, opened their sharp-toothed mouths wide, directing high frequency sonar towards the hull hovering above them. Reeling back in pain as the powerful waves pounded against the receptive flesh of my jaw and neck, I felt Father grasp for me, and we floundered together, struggling to stay upright.

Shoals of fish around us pulsed, breaking apart into their individual fragments at the distortion. I was nearly at the point of passing out when, finally, the sonic vibrations stilled. Above us, and to the side of the boat's hull, the water became disturbed, thrashing and churning as those aboard tried to maneuver the vessel away, using flattened poles to push through the water.   Before they could, three of the Sirens ascended air-ward, leeching themselves to the side of the craft, each tail thrashing briefly before disappearing over the side of the boat and into the glare of the dry world.

Father pulled away from me, commanding me to stay where I was. I watched as he joined the remaining four Sirens as they attached themselves to the bottom of the boat, stabbing their brutal obsidian blades into the underside of the vessel, rending jagged punctures along the pithy material of the hull. Streams of air bubbles cascaded from multiple rents and the boat began to spin and pitch. Vague noises, high and muffled, trembled down to me from the surface, and a few thin skeins of blood unwound delicately in the water above. It drifted in fragile spirals that spooled around my outstretched hands far below. Horrified and fascinated, I swam closer.

The noises from the boat coalesced into high pitched shouts and screams. I felt their vibrations in my flesh in the seconds before the first body tumbled into the blue.   Five more followed in quick succession, hanging still for a moment in the waves before starting their slow slide to the sea bed.   The Sirens who had boarded the craft slipped back into the water after them, sliding into the current, two of them supporting an injured third.   This third was bearing her many rows of teeth in a silent rictus of agony.   A terrible wound in the side of her neck had exposed her gill arches, and the filaments gushed purple-red pulses that wound around her companions like cuttlefish ink.

The boat, foundering, began to slip beneath the waves.   Father and the other Sirens, so distracted with the wrecking craft and the injured member of their party, did not notice me insinuate myself towards the un-folk things – the humans - that danced down bonelessly towards the sea bed, trailing torn skin and tattered clothing. They did not notice me touch the first one, or see me recoil in horror when I felt his segmented lower body, divided into two thick trunks, just as in Grandmother's stories. He was dead. Around his neck, glinted an ornament on a metal chain, and I pulled it free, wrapping it tightly around my wrist. I moved on to the next creature. Four more, also dead, also wearing the same talisman around their necks on chains of varying materials and thicknesses; I took each bauble and then let the tides resume their sluggish pull on the bodies.

I heard Father's shout, distantly, as I came to the last one. A sudden tug of current had dragged the final corpse far from the gracelessly plummeting boat, and I had followed it, so that Father and the Sirens were just remote flickering forms. But as I neared this body, it suddenly thrashed, a volcano of air bubbles erupting from its nose and mouth, its arms pumping clumsily and its bizarre tail-limbs kicking, pushing for the dry world above. I flinched backwards in alarm. The human's eyes, wide open and frantic, fixed on mine, and for a heartbeat, we saw each other clearly. And then he was gone, flailing for the surface, pummeling the water roughly and leaving a stream of adrenaline in his wake that washed into my glands in a heady ripple.

Behind me, I sensed someone approaching, fast. The human was just about to break into the dry air when my father swam past me and barreled upwards, grabbing the lone survivor by his non-tail and pulling him back down into the depths.

"Father!" I shouted. "What are you doing!"

"Go back to the Keep!" he bellowed, pure rage in his eyes.

"But he cannot hurt us – he is but one, his comrades are all dead…"

Father, holding the weakly thrashing thing tight in his almighty arms, brought the obsidian blade from his belt and drew the serrated edge across his captive's throat. A bright wash of blood churned out in a cloud that obscured both their faces, and the thing that was not of the sea folk became limp, its legs drifting in the strong strand of the tide, its arms hanging against my father's body.

"Now he cannot hurt us," said my father grimly. The rage in his eyes had clarified and hardened to something else, and I could not look at it, or him, a moment longer. I pushed back and swam, hard, past the Sirens and the sunken boat, back to the Nest with its ripening mothers, and beyond it. I swam until, at the edge of the commune, I found Grandmother floating where I had left her, looking into the cloud murkened waters as if waiting for my return. She took one look at my face and inhaled sharply.

I did not explain what had happened, instead pulling the tangle of chains from my wrist and thrusting it at her.

"What are these, Grandmother? What do they mean?" My voice was not steady.

She looked at them and reached out a hand that shook slightly to touch the chains and the ornaments attached to each: two tiny bars, one vertical, one horizontal, intersecting. She drew her fingers back as if they had been burnt in a hydrothermal vent.

"These are their souls."

"What are souls?"

Grandmother looked past me, straining her eyes into the darkening waters.

"What are souls!" I repeated, frantic.

"Your Father is coming," she said. She curled my fingers into a ball around the chains and their hanging souls. "Hide these."

I kissed her quickly on the cheek and pushed forwards for the Keep.

Severance

Chapter 3

I was confined to the Keep, of course. Two moons fattened and faded and still I was kept tight within the walls of coral and anemone, watching through slits as the stars appeared and wheeled overhead. I thought, always, of the human and how his blood had exploded into the water so that I felt its warmth kiss the coldness of my upper body, a small breath against the silvery skin of my stomach and breasts.

Grandmother was not permitted to visit me. But Sephona came once; my cool eyed, black haired sister who, on this occasion, couldn't quite feign her usual regal disinterest.

"What have you done?" she hissed excitedly, looking over her shoulder at the archway as if fearful of Father's appearance. I wondered if she had, in fact, been given permission to see me at all. We are none of us, my sisters and I, entirely without a rebellious streak.

"I was there, Seph. When the Sirens brought the boat down. There was a ….one of them was not dead. Father…"

"A human! Was it hideous?" She shuddered, a small smile pulling at her lips. "Did you touch it?"

"Listen to me, Sephona," I whispered. "The boat that sank. It looked like the fossil wrecks beyond the cordons. Do you understand what that means?"

"That a few of the Old Ones have survived. And returned. I am not stupid." She flicked a skein of hair from her face, and it floated in a soft drift to mingle with my own. "And what of it?"

I caught her face in my hands. "They were not diseased."

A noise outside startled us both and I dropped my hands and pushed back from my sister. She gave me a crooked smile and, then slid out of the room and into the tunnel that led down from the tower and back to the Keep's central suites. The noise rose in pitch and volume, and I realized it was coming from beyond the Keep, the sound of a great mass of the folk converging outside the walls. Complex eddies streamed into my chamber from below, carrying a wash of voices that echoed and bubbled against every surface. The folk feel sound as much as hear it, and the rumble and roar of the congregation battered and buffeted me like a riptide. I hurtled to the uppermost reaches of my tower prison and peered through one of the watch slits.

Sure enough, a crowd had gathered just beyond the great gates. They were calling out, anger and fear pumping from them, polluting the water with hormones so that I, too, high up in my cage, began to feel the communal distress below and respond to it in kind. The people called for answers, for reassurances: Had we been exposed to corruption? Were our children safe? Would the creatures come again? What was to be done? I realized I, too, had unwillingly joined in the mass clamour. When the gates swung open and my father appeared with a phalanx of guards, he looked up at me in my prison and saw me screaming with the crowd. Fighting the rush of chemicals that infused me, I clamped my mouth shut and pulled slow drafts of water through my gills. Against the tide of surging hormones, I willed the slowing of my heart.

Father spoke to the gathered sea-folk calmly. The mass quieted. He told them he had called a council at the Nest come sunset, and would speak then about what had happened, and how our safety was to be maintained in the future.

"We are in no danger," he finished, "the humans were carefully inspected, and their bodies showed no sign of corruption. We also checked their apparel and all parts of their craft for radiation. The whole was clean."

"What if more come?" a lone voice shouted at Father's retreating back, but he had already passed the threshold of the Keep, and two of his guards pulled the great doors shut behind him. The crowd, cowed, drifted away to their various duties.

I would not be permitted to attend the meeting, of course.

I slipped my fingers into one of the small crevices in the tower wall. The tendril of an anemone brushed my skin, softly probing, as I brought my tangled chain of souls from the hole. I contemplated it for a long time, thinking of the dead creatures – humans – and of Farner, too, lost in the waters beyond the realm. A suspicion took root in my mind, like the red flower in the salty shale of my garden: improbable, irresistible, and striving from the deep, for the clear light beyond the waves.

For the remainder of my long confinement, I nursed these thoughts, tending them like a precious harvest. I ate sparingly of the coralline algae and pulped sea whip that one guard or other bought me four times a day. I smoothed my fins and scales with kelp butter when I woke, and, through my days, worked a mosaic on the floor of my tower room, dropping shards of amber, beads of jet, and splinters of pearl that pattered and coalesced like the spots of rain that fell, often now, on the surface of the sea above, sending down gentle little shocks and ripples to the folk below. By the time the pattern beneath me neared completion and my punishment approached its end, a terrible conclusion had formed in my mind.

It was Amonie who came to end my imprisonment.

"You are free," she said, simply.

I pulled her to me in a fierce embrace. Amonie was dear to me, and I had not seen her face for the life and death of two moon shifts.

"What news is there?" I said, releasing her at last. "Have there been sightings of more boats? The guards will tell me nothing."

Amonie looked at me strangely. "Why would there be more boats? Father says the humans that wrecked were the last of their kind. And they are all dead. They cannot harm us."

A low anger surged through me, hearing my sister parrot back Father's words so obediently.

"Amonie! This is nonsense! How could a band of five possibly comprise the sum total of a species? Father is wrong. There are more. There has to be."

She looked uneasy.

"What does Grandmother say of this?" I asked. "Never mind," I embraced her once more, a quick squeeze of shoulder and scale. "I will ask her myself."

I swam from the tower, gliding past the guards and shaking off my captivity like so many clinging barnacles. Full of my own freedom, I rose in a sweeping spiral through the layers of water, corkscrewing to the surface in a slick slide of wake to explode into the air. Gills sucking feebly, I pushed my hair back from my eyes and rose my face to the sun, feeling its terrible burn and the salt whip of the wind. Breathless, with lungs on fire, I arched my back and tunneled once more into the waves, my skin raw from the sting of the unfiltered light.

Barreling back down to the sea bed, I passed the bivalve fields; one of the workers there nudged his fellow and lifted his chin towards me as I passed above. They exchanged some words, following me with their eyes as I swam over the neat nests of clam, scallop and mussel, each little 'farm' feeding a complex array of siphons and cracked sponges.

"Have you seen my Grandmother?" I called to the staring pair.

"At the infirmary, Miss," one said. His words were respectful, but the amused glint in his eye was not.

I hovered near them. "The infirmary? She has been taken ill?"

"One of the Sirens nears death. Your Grandmother tends her."

I thought of the wounded Siren who had boarded the boat so many tides ago. My mind filled with the drawn out days of her slow death and I felt my gorge rise. Unable to speak, I nodded to the farm hands and pushed away, my body moving in swift ripples as I passed through the centre of the commune. Skimming the borders of the pleasure gardens and moving past the great metal-works, the steam from the hydrothermal vent it was built upon billowed up from its many stacks, as I made my way to the honeycombed caves of the infirmary.

Sure enough, my Grandmother was within, tucked tight inside one of the central chambers. Glass squids, suspended in cages from ceiling and wall, emitted a delicate bioluminescence that lit my Grandmother's face in fragile shades of blue and yellow. She was bent over the terribly wounded Siren, pressing a poultice of coral-farmed secosteroids to the ragged hole in the Siren's throat.

"Grandmother?" I whispered into the hush.

She did not turn to me but spoke, instead, to the unconscious Siren, her words but a low ripple through the water. "My Granddaughter has many questions for me, I think, Aglaope. She must wait yet."

"Can she not be saved?" I asked, coming closer to the bed of sea grass and brown algae.

My Grandmother still did not turn to face me.

"Can the Elders not heal her?" I pressed.

"She is beyond that, my love."

A sudden thought effervesced through my mind, bright as a trail of phyto-plankton on a moonlit night. "Can the souls help her? The things I found on the humans?"

"Did they help the humans that wore them, child? No. Their blood spilled out regardless and their hearts stilled and cooled. Finally, she turned her head to face me. "Their souls can only help them after their death. They lead their keepers to a life beyond this one."

My mind reeled. "A life after death? So if...after Aglaope's body dissolves, one of the souls could make her rise again?"

43

"No. The souls you have taken belong only to the men who bore them around their necks. Only if they are returned can their onward journeys commence."

Air bubbles hissed sluggishly from the great rent in the Siren's neck. It escaped in a tainted stream that rose to the ceiling of the cavern, where the light from the glass squids sparked tiny crystals from Aglaope's final breaths. I put my fingers to her forehead, and felt a shocking warmth there. I remembered that she was but eighty years old.

"We must make one for her, then, Grandmother. A soul."

She ran a gentle hand along my dorsal and adipose fins, smoothing them in calming circles with her jeweled fingers. "The soul resides within the metal; it is not of it. We have long lost the skill to craft such things."

My brain buzzed and, with an effort, I focused on the questions I needed to ask.

"Grandmother. The cordons. We have always been told that danger lies beyond them. Radiation exposure. Disease. Corruption of the folk. Yet...Farner went to the landmass and returned unharmed. He did not sicken. And the humans that came...they were not tainted, and neither were the Sirens or Father, despite having contact with them. I need to know..."

My Grandmother interrupted me. "You do not need to know."

"But I think..."

"Fetch the Second Elder – quickly! Aglaope passes."

I glanced at the Siren before hurrying from the chamber. Beads of blood flickered in a ragged spume of air that churned in a sporadic stream from smashed filaments of her gill. Her chest hitched and drew in, the skin sucking back against her ribs and upper abdomen in a terrible concavity. I slid from the small cavern, swimming through the endless maze of tunnels, until I came to the Hub, calling for the Second Elder even as I approached the driftwood portal. She appeared, gliding out to meet me, her eyes calm and clear.

"It is Aglaope," I said, breathless.

She put a hand briefly to my shoulder before skimming swiftly back along the tunnel from which I had come.

"Wait!" I called, propelling myself forward.

The Second Elder turned her head, but did not slow. "You are to return home. It is not for you to witness a dissolution."

I pushed my tail back against my own wake, slowing and stopping at a turn in the tunnels in time to see the Second Elder disappear around the next bend. A blood-red resolve began to bloom in my mind. I left the Hub, the questions I had harboured throughout my long confinement burning wickedly in my mind. I made for the Crystal Keep. And my father.

Severance

Chapter 4

I had not always been such a disappointment to my sire. When I was just a child, twenty years or thereabouts, he called courage what he now calls recklessness, and esteemed my curiosity as a brightness of intellect. Grandmother knew differently, though. She has always seen me, and into me, and I think that is why I am her favourite. She envies my strangeness, and has always known, I believe, that I would be more in need of her guidance than my sisters. Not to subvert my stubbornness, you understand, but to quietly encourage it. But I see something in her eyes that I see in my own when the moon is high and my reflection glitters, brittle, on the millpond sea; and I recognize it.

I found my father in high state, presiding over a small council in the Lower Hall. He glanced up and, seeing me lingering at the portal, flicked me away with a curt wave of his hand. "We will speak later," he told me, before turning his attention back to his ministers and the head of the guard.

"Please excuse my daughter," he said to them, lightly. "She has much to learn in the way of statecraft."

They tittered obediently. My father looked up once more and gave me a small, indulgent smile, before motioning to the attendant who stood beside the portal to seal the room. With me outside of it.

I put my forehead to the craggy wall of the passageway in frustration. I pounded it gently a few times against the crust of coral and anemone, feeling it give, slightly, beneath the pressure of my skull. I sensed a presence approaching and turned to see my sister, Sephona, gliding towards me. Her face was lined with grimness, but her eyes spoke a different story. They glittered, and a grin lurked within them. "Free at last, Sister?"

"Sephona, Aglaope has died."

"I know it." Her lips pulled down in a sad line. Sephona has always had a morbid love of the dramatic and the tragic. At a distance. "A messenger has just brought the news to the Keep. Father must be told." She paused. "Wait, you already knew of this?"

I ignored the question. "Father is within," I motioned to the closed portal. "In council. I have already been evicted. You must wait."

My sister rolled her eyes at me, and hammered firmly at the door. The attendant pulled it open from within, the water from inside and outside the chamber rushing together and erupting in a small wash of turbulence. Seeing Sephona, the attendant snapped to attention.

"Miss?"

"An urgent message has arrived for my father. I must see him immediately."

"But he is in council, Miss. He must not be disturbed." The attendant lowered his voice. "He is dealing with most urgent matters."

Sephona brushed past him and swept into the chamber. I heard her brusque voice within as I remained in the passageway. A few moments later, Father swam out, tight faced, and tailed by his ministerial congregation. My sister followed after. As she passed me, she turned.

"I have spoken with Amonie; with Clista and Kelan, too." She was close to my face, and spoke quickly and quietly. "You seek something, Sister. It disturbs us all." She stroked my hair. "Perhaps the answers lie here." She pulled something from the chain around her neck. It glowed dully next to the small globes of manganese and pearls of olivine that dripped down her throat in opalescent clusters, where it had been disguised. She pressed the key into my hand, imprinting it painfully into the skin of my palm, before twice whipping her tail and undulating away from me in our father's wake.

I looked at the key in my palm. I recognized the black symbols engraved on its surface. It would allow access to a chamber in the Lower Pit. A prickle of unease sidestepped, crab-like, up my spine. I wondered at its being in Sephona's possession. I should have considered this more. I know that now. Instead, baffled, I emerged and rose up from the Keep, letting myself be carried on the tidal eddies that swirled around the fortress. A drift tugged me towards the surface, pulling me until I lay just below the tabletop of the waves. The sun and clouds floated, watery and wavery, just above me. I reached up my arm and touched the underside of the surface, so that, at the slightest increase of pressure, my fingers would burst through into the air while I remained, prone, beneath it.

I thought hard about pushing sky-ward and flinging the key far from me. I felt a strong compulsion to do it and yet, yet…I did not.

Instead, I closed my fingers in a tight ball around it, shut my eyes, and drifted there on the cusp of air and water, before turning and pointing like a spear for the sea bed. I shot down, fast, arrowing through the heart of a shoal of scrub tetra that scattered and re-formed in my wake. Like a wound, closing in on itself. A voice called out to me as I skimmed the algae and sand and upthrust rocks, clearing jagged fingers of ancient obsidian and sulfide by a mere hair's breadth. I ignored the voice, despite recognizing the fear in Amonie's tone. I sped onwards.

The Pit was far from the main commune, all the way out near the northern cordons, and by the time I reached it, I was exhausted. After two moons cooped up in my tower, I had spent most of the day swimming aimlessly. My spinal column ached with the exertion, and my caudal fin spasmed in a sporadic pulse that matched my heartbeat. I rested briefly, gathering my resolve, calcifying it around me like a stone sheath And then I dived down into the chasm that split the sea bed like a jagged cut that has penetrated to the bone.

Nothing grew in the Pit. Its walls, widening as it deepened, were not lined with weed or kelp, and neither clam nor mollusc nor barnacle clung to its sides. It was an arid throat that plunged into the hard flesh of the earth's crust. The waters quickly darkened as I sank lower, yet I could still make out the dull iridescence of the blooms of chalcanthite that clung to the flanks of the ravine in poisonous nests. Indispensable in keeping the Pit's few residents docile, they threw their toxins into the drop so that, I quickly felt sleepy and calm. I slowed, stopped. Floated limply between the dead lips of the chasm, wondering what I was doing, and marveling at my recklessness. How could I have doubted Father, or Grandmother, even? I could not remember what my purpose was in being here, many fathoms deep, in the stomach of the Pit.

Just as I was on the verge of pushing back to the upper ocean, a thought exploded in my mind: the creature, the human, from the wrecked boat, his blood bright in the water. His eyes, that had seen into mine. The force of the image drove out, for a moment, the chalcanthite fug from my brain. Before I could lose my resolve again, I hurtled down, in a frantic blast, to the Lower Chambers of the Pit.

I stopped at the first steel door, one of a number that pocked the walls of the ravine, maybe four or five in all. Few cells were required, as it was extremely rare for a member of the folk to commit a crime so heinous that permanent incarceration in the Pit was passed down as judgement. It had not happened in my lifetime; and though I am sixty years old, I am young, for the folk are long lived. I turned Sephona's key over in my hand. On one side were the glyphs signifying the Pit. On the other was a different, single symbol. I looked from it to the steel door embedded in the bare rock. There was a symbol carved above the door, and it did not match the one on the key. I crossed to the other side of the chasm, where another door was sunk into the rock. No match there, either. A low moan escaped from the closed metal mouth; a moan that rose in jagged ascensions to become a demented giggle.

Swiftly, I swam downwards to the next cell, feeling again the pull of the chalcanthite on my wits. Here, the symbol scratched into the rock matched that on the key. Suddenly, the waters around me darkened further as a pod of dolphacs spiraled in the clearer currents far above. Like a cloud passing, their shadow receded and, when it was gone, a shaft of sunlight penetrated at a jagged angle. It lit the unfathomable depths of the Pit in a filtered glow that faded and disappeared into the vastness yet beneath me. I felt a yawning vertigo, and clung tightly to the rock.

Was I actually going to do this? I wondered, even as I watched my own hand move the key toward the lock in the centre of the door. I wondered, even as I saw my fingers turn the metal in the slot and heard a great clanking of gears somewhere deep in the ancient mechanism. Wondered whether I might not actually be safe and dreaming in my bed in the Coral Keep. But when I withdrew the key and the door swung open, spewing air bubbles around me so that I was blinded, I fully understood what I had done. A rush of pure panic shot through me, and I nearly passed out from the force of it.

I pushed against the outrush of air, gripped the sides of the door, and tried to push it closed again with all my might. I thought I would manage it, but just before it swung shut, steel glinting through the shaft of sunlight that still shone down in a broken beam, an arm emerged from the total blackness within. The arm was not silver-blue, like my own – like all the folk – but armeria pink, like those belonging to the human creatures. And it was incredibly strong. I pushed harder, straining my flagging muscles and fins to their breaking point, and yet the door did not close. The arm was joined by another. All at once, the door exploded open, my strength overpowered, and I was hurled back against the opposite wall of the chasm. I cried out in fear and pain as I felt my dorsal fin become impaled on a thick needle of sulfide. I struggled to escape, but could not, and feared I would cause terrible damage if I tried to rip myself free by force.

The open door gaped on the other side of the chasm. Streams of air bubbles escaped from within, rising to the surface like floating strands of pearls. The strange pink arms had disappeared, but I felt a presence within the chamber, watching me. I struggled again, and screamed out when I felt my dorsal tear further. Droplets of blood clouded the water, swirling around me, and I felt an awful darkness begin to descend on my mind and body.

That was when the woman emerged from her prison. She glided to me, her twin tails undulating through the water like a pair of serpents, and laid a soft pink hand to my cheek. Her smile dazzled me.

"Don't fret and fever, Sweet," she said, soft and low, into my ear. "I can give you what you seek."

I struggled for clarity, trying to push the poison from my brain by sheer force of will. "You don't know what it is I seek," I panted.

The woman reached behind me and, with a delicate twist of her wrist, released me from the spike of sulfide.

"Freedom. Of course," she said.

Severance

Chapter 5

Grandmother said our kind had retreated to the swamps and marshes of the near dead world after the Ravage, when the sun swam in a murky, scum filled pond of a sky and the air was hot steam, fetid and dust corrupted. Grandmother said the Old Ones were as extinct as the mythical great lizards, and the pollinating insects. She would tell my sisters and I of these insects, how they floated through the sky like fish, resting only to suck the sweet warm blood from the blooms of that lost place. And she'd speak of The Old Ones, the land walkers. How we, the folk, were their devolution and evolution incarnate. Their downfall and their rise from the nuclear ashes.

Grandmother said that the dry lands, are now vast and empty, covered in dog-scrub and mutant foliage that strangles any vestigial remnant of indigenous plant life. That only terrible beasts walk the baked earth, three eyed tumorous horrors and slouching hybrids that eat their own offspring. She said the flowers have long since died.

Grandmother whispered that the waters had protected us – the folk. That the plankton and protozoa had absorbed much of the radiation that had infected the rest of the earth. It left a dead carpet of cells on the ocean's surface many fingers thick, in the weeks and years after the Ravage, that stank and reeked and kept the sea's upper layers in twilight for more turns of the tides than could be counted. And Grandmother told us how the folk, slowly *becoming* as the centuries and eons spun by, moved from their bogs and mud shallows to find pockets of safety in the deeper waters. Safe zones where the mineral make-up of the rock strata provided a near total shield for the residual filth that yet contaminated the sea.

Grandmother said all of these things. But she was wrong.

I had sensed the salt in the stories even as a young child. Farner had, too. He was the only one I knew who was...like me. When we were little, we spent hours at the cordons, our small fingers wrapped tight around the smooth flex of the wire, staring at the great space beyond. Straining our eyes to see the fossil wrecks through the shifting currents, pushing our hands through the gaps until the circulating blood stalled and prickled, and our fingers became numb. Yet still we *stretched* into that great unknown. Occasionally, a friend or two would join us at the boundary, pushing and laughing and nudging. Once, as a rare whale passed beyond our borders, vast and sedate, Farner said that it looked neither three eyed nor tumorous. And the friends with us looked at Farner crookedly and laughed. But I did not. His words watered a seed that had fallen into my mind long since.

I asked Grandmother about it one night, after she'd sung to me of the coves and caverns of the rainbow seas, kissing my gills and forehead until I giggled a stream of bubbles that caught the moon's light seeping into my chamber window.

"The ocean is healing," she told me. "But the ancient human cells we carry could yet be corrupted by traces of the poison that are still present in the water and lands beyond our Realm."

But when she told me this, her voice had become a flat monotone, as if she were speaking by rote, and wanted me to know it. "This is known," she finished, a gleam in her eye.

"Known by who?" I asked.

She had leaned in close to me, then. "There is death beyond the cordons," she said.

My young eyes grew wide.

"But maybe not yours, my love."

And now, as I lie here and tell you this story, I can't help but think, with an affectionate bitterness, if there can be such a thing. That Grandmother was terminally wrong about so much.

When Farner's parents caught tide of the time we were spending together at the nets, and heard the rumours that he may have been responsible for the breach that had appeared overnight in a cordon in the eighth quadrant – a ragged, burnt ended hole in the razor tipped wire maybe half the length of a child's tail - they sent him to work in the Fissure, mining manganese. And I was banned from seeing him again.

But I used to slide from the Keep, sometimes, in the churned light of the pre-dawn, to lurk in the reefs that fringed the Fissure, trying to catch a glimpse of him there. He saw me, though not always. We never spoke. But it was only a matter of time. Hence my forced presence in the courtroom. Hence the flower. Hence my incarceration. We are bound to our joined fates, Farner and I.

And so, leading in a direct path from all of this, I found myself bleeding and intoxicated in the bowel of the Pit, staring into the eyes of the most hideous and beautiful creature I had ever encountered. The twin ridges of my jaw were held tight within her grasp and I was unsure whether I desired to escape or surrender to seduction.

"You look just like your mother," she said, turning my head to one side and then the other. "Yes. The very spitting image."

"You knew my mother?" I said, the words emerging as a tarry slur.

The two-tailed woman dropped her hand from my face.

"Maybe. Or perhaps I'm mistaking you for someone else. You wouldn't believe the number of visitors I get." She made a noise that was the simulacrum of a laugh, but there was no joy in it, nor even cynical amusement. It was the empty and hollow cackle of someone who has not known sanity for a long time, and it broke the spell that held me fixed in place.

I swam upwards, fast, the mind-shattering laughter following me along The Pit's stone gullet. It vibrated off the walls and insinuated itself into the pores of my skin and the vitrodentine of my scales. It was unbearable. Finally, I reached the top and collapsed on my back on the sea bed, gills laboring and heart pounding. The chalcanthite fur in my brain immediately began to fragment and disperse in the clear waters, and the magnitude of what I had done would have overcome me if I hadn't been so totally spent. Far overhead, the sun was setting, and the undersides of the waves were the orange-green of the rusted out fossil wrecks beyond the cordons. I could sense their run and splash as the breakers built in a strengthening wind. A storm approached. I could taste it in the almost imperceptible fizz of the current, and in the bursts of adrenaline released by the passing fish that sought shelter.

Inevitably, the strong pink arms appeared over the lip of the abyss, and the woman-creature hauled herself over its rim to flop onto the sand as if she could not swim at all. I wondered if she was mocking me. The twin trunks of her tails pulsed thickly around her in the shale. There seemed little point in fleeing. And who could protect me, after all? Could I truly admit to my father what I had done? To my Grandmother? My blood thinned in my veins at the very thought.

So we lay side by side, this woman and I, my eyes wide and fixed on the heaving water above, hers closed in languorous release. Time passed, and the amber tints leached from the Realm as darkness fell.

The wind, sky side, had whipped the waves into white crested frenzies, and I felt the push and pull of their giant breaths from where I lay beneath them.

"What are you?" I said at last.

"Is it not obvious?" she answered. "Is my tail not a clue? Has your family's in-breeding dulled your wits, child? It is a less unattractive affliction, I grant you, than two heads."

I couldn't help but look pointedly at her double tail, weaving close to me. Seeing my regard, she smiled widely.

"You think the pot calls the kettle black?"

"Why were you imprisoned?" I asked, returning my gaze to the dark layers of water around and above us, and the darker night beyond. The few cages of glass squids, attached by chains to the Pit's entrance, provided the only light, a wide and diffuse glow that spread across the sea bed in a white-gold fan.

She turned onto her stomach and looked at me with huge blue eyes. Her hair had been carelessly hacked so that it floated in short russet curls around her cheeks and chin. I had never seen such a lovely face in my life.

"You really haven't been told about me, have you?" She barked a short laugh and rolled onto her back once again. "You truly don't know!"

"I know I never should have set you free," I said.

"Such a thing to say! And knowing not a thing about me. I've a mind to withhold my services."

I knew I should probably swim as fast as my battered adipose fin could bear in the opposite direction; any direction. Even one that could take me into my father's presence and, most likely, half a lifetime of incarceration in my tower. Or banishment. But I didn't.

"Services?" I said instead.

"I owe you a favour, Dear Heart. As you pointed out, you have freed me from a most grievous situation. You have restored my very life, you could say."

"I want nothing from you, unless you have a mind to return yourself to your cell and let me lock it behind you."

She did not laugh this time. She turned her head instead, so that her cheek pressed against the small stones of the sea bed, and sought my eyes. Incredibly, I found I could not resist the force of her will. Despite my best efforts to keep my gaze on the twin darkness of sea and sky above, I, too, turned to meet her stare.

"A life for a life," she said. "What is freely granted may be taken back again if that is the wish of the giver. Should you will it, I shall return myself to The Pit to live out the remainder of my years – half as long as the lifespans enjoyed by the folk, as you may have guessed; and that's nothing to do with the appalling food. You can go back to The Keep, sitting in at court sessions, visiting new mothers, waiting to be married off and, let me guess…making mosaics on your bedroom floor. How sweet."

I found that I could not speak.

"But you don't want to, do you? She shuffle-slid across the few hand-spans of sand that separated us until the length of one of her tails pressed against my own She spoke softly into my ear. "You thought your heart would break, didn't you, when you saw him fade into the blues and indigos beyond the cordons on the day of the banishment. He did not swim away, though, did he? You did. And it was only when you finally looked back, from a great distance, that you saw him flick his tail and turn slowly, spinning away into the great places beyond the Realm. Because he had been waiting, hadn't he?

To see if you ever looked back at him. His little princess."

"I am no princess," I managed, but my throat was closed so tightly that even those few words almost choked me. "How could you know these things? Who are you?"

"I have been called many things," she said. "My mother gave me one name, my father another. Your own father called me a witch. Which is probably why he sentenced me to the cells. Traditionally, the punishment for witchcraft is drowning. Ironic, really." And she flicked her twin tails and ascended to the surface and the storm that raged there.

And, souls help me, I followed.

Severance

Chapter 6

Her name was Persephone, and this is the story she told me. Not then, of course, but later. During my…recovery.

"My father was of the folk," she had said.

I couldn't respond then, obviously.

"But my mother was from sky-side. So I am both air and water, earth and sea."

I looked at her legs that were also tails. Her tails that were almost legs. She saw me looking and smiled. I returned it. Painfully.

"My father was steward to yours" she continued. "No, he was more than that. A loyal liege man of more than two centuries, upholding the supremacy of your kin, even in the face of rebellion. They had grown up together in the Keep and were dear, each to the other. My father was an orphan of that rebellion: his own parents had died in the defence of yours. So close were they, in fact, that my father was privy to certain…truths. Was a part of covert…operations.

"Let me be clear. He was a Wrecker.

"He and the other Wreckers would lure human boats close to the Realm, using moonlight and mirrors to send false signals from leagues distant, and then the Sirens would be sent to dispatch them. It's how he met my mother. Not the most romantic of stories, I'm afraid.

"To what purpose, you ask, this Wrecking?"

I had not said a word – how could I? – yet she must have read the question in my eyes.

"The reasons were twofold. The first was the accumulation of material and wealth. You surely must have questioned the level of technology enjoyed by the folk in this watery little world? You cannot think all of this can have been dredged up from the ocean's guts? How hilarious! This piracy has been going on for eons, darling. The folk would be little more than mutated fish, swimming aimlessly in their own befouled little patch of pond, if they hadn't been despoiling the crafts and sciences of their human cousins since those same cousins raised their heads above the parapet of their wounded world.

"And the second reason? Sport."

I must have looked appalled. Who wouldn't?

"I know, Dear Heart: beastly." She paused. "But perhaps understandable. Hunting for pleasure has long been part of the human psyche, and blood always outs in the end. Our long dead ancestors hunted lions, did you know that? Fearsome four-legged beasts of fur and hot flesh. Of course, the status quo has had to be maintained these many millennia: power springs from ignorance, control from obedience, the old 'it is known, it is known' mantra. So utterly unoriginal. Your father and those before him feared and still fear the human world. They fear the loss of their dominion. It has ever been the lot of lords and kings and leaders, to tremble at the thought of the diminishment of their power. Thus the cordons and the official line that humanity – the pure kind – had been all but destroyed air-side. As I know you suspect, the waters beyond the Realm, and the landmasses beyond that, are no more corrupt than I am." She laughed then, the familiar insane giggle. "A bad analogy, I grant you. They are as innocent of corruption as your dear young Farner."

I struggled to sit upright.

"Easy now," she soothed. "I misspoke. It is a habit of mine. I repent. I meant only that the outside waters and the lands they lick are as untainted as they were before the Ravage. The sun now paddles in an aseptic sky and the earth puts forth green shoots.

"And red flowers."

She watched me closely. I lay back down and kept my expression neutral. My trust had not been included in the terms of our bargain.

"But we must return to the heartwarming tale of how my father nearly murdered my mother. She was on a ship that the Wreckers had brought in, and set to die like all the others aboard, her fate to waltz down to the ocean's floor in a flurry of fine linen and torn flesh. The Sirens' work is hardly elegant, darling, is it?

"My father saw her, wavering through the water's lens, held half overboard and throat gripped in a Siren's hand. And when he noticed the obsidian blade about to journey into her chest cavity and her blood about to spill into the waves, he found himself at the mercy of a most powerfully persuasive emotion.

"He saved her, you see. He saw something he recognized in her eyes. You know this feeling, no? She had blue eyes. Like me. Our paths converge,

Child. For you, too, have looked full in the face of a human in the moments before his breath stopped and he drifted down to the bottom like a storm-caught stingray to become a waterlogged corpse. I have seen that it is so.

"Yet that was not my mother's destiny. For my father took her. He killed the Siren with her own obsidian blade, pulling it from the outer layers of my mother's flesh so that a thin stream of blood splashed into the water with them as they tumbled from the sinking boat. He swam beyond the cordons with her, to an island that was known to him, and that he had long kept secret from deep instinct. He lay her on the muddy sand and panted in the shallows, beached and doomed by his love for her.

"And when your father and the Sirens found them, some weeks later, my father was already dead: the untreated wounds inflicted on him in the deadly struggle with my mother's would-be killer had festered in the shallows. My mother yet lived. With me a seed within her. And she was taken back to your father.

I wonder if you can guess the rest."

Persephone moved from my bed to the half-submerged window, fringed with molluscs and the semi-calcified remains of long dead creatures, pushing herself up on her tails to gaze at the sea beyond, opalescent in the early morning light. I turned onto my side, drugged sleep pawing at my mind. Persephone waded to my side through the shallows. She cupped her hands to sluice salt water over my body, and rubbed kelp butter into the drying, cracked skin of my tail and upper fins.

With infinite tenderness, she untied the dressings on the side of my neck, then packed the open wounds there with fresh seaweed before re-applying clean linen bandages that wrapped around my throat like a strangler's hands, so tight that I couldn't have screamed with the pain in any case. I registered what she did only vaguely, as though my mind was attached to my body by the flimsiest of threads, and was floating at a great distance from my physical form, threatening to untether completely at any moment.

Persephone's words, though, soaked into the secret folds of my brain just as the poultice she applied to my outraged flesh permeated to the raw layers of meat below – insidious and irresistibly soothing.

"My mother was kept in a sea cave much like this one," she continued. "Without the view, sadly. She was guarded day and night by a Wrecker or a Siren. Marooned far from land as she was, she had no chance of escape.

"Your father visited her, though. Many times."

Through drooping eyelids, on the brink of being washed away on a tide of crystallized dimethyl sulphide, I watched my companion shin through the low water of the sweating hole in the rock where we dwelt to a rusted metal spike that had been hammered into the far wall. From it hung many souls: some of metal, some of wood, some that glittered like pure white ice. She fingered them gently, bringing first one, then another, to her lips. She closed her eyes as she kissed each of them.

"And they waited for me to spawn." Her voice came from a great distance, the wind muffled cry of a lone gull. "When I came into the world, your father, seeing what I was, promptly had my mother killed, her birthing blood still staining the rocks on which she lay.

"I was assigned a nurse and guards of my own. Lucky me. And kept imprisoned safely beyond the cordons for years that I have counted, but that need not concern you."

The small illumination that trickled into my slitted eyes, swollen with impending sleep, faded and was almost lost. The last thing I saw before my consciousness broke free of its bonds was – I dearly hope – an illusion. For there was Persephone, bringing one of the chain-hung souls from its spike and taking it, whole, into her mouth. It's horizontal cross section pushed obscenely against the insides of her cheeks, threatening to puncture the very flesh. In that moment, her beauty fled, and only her emptiness remained.

The soul. It was as if she were eating it.

***

For maybe ten tides' turns, I woke and slept in a fevered cycle of lucid dreaming and dream-like waking. I lay, throughout this unmarked time, on a flat-topped rock that breached the shallow waters of our cavern like the belly of a beached whale. I breathed raggedly through my mouth, each inward pull agony, each outward exhalation as if the air being passed was hydro-thermal vent super-heated and scalding my innards as it fled my throat. My lungs, at first, pitched and heaved and spasmed like a storm tide but, as the days and hours passed, seemed to become resigned to their new state of being.

Still, the dreams were worse. I dreamt of Farner. I was always at the cordon. I sought him with my gaze, sweeping the waters beyond the net with wide eyes as if he would have lingered there all this time, waiting for me. The mesh shimmered, flexing innocently as if it wouldn't turn to razors at a pressure greater than the push of a small child's hand. The moon above threw down a bony shimmer that glanced off my body and the pig chrome of the struts that supported the cordons, burrowing into the seabed in a marching line that disappeared in the dim.

And then, Farner was there. A fin's breadth away, hovering just beyond the boundary. But when he opened his mouth to speak, no words came. We were both mute, staring at each other in horror, our mouths hinge-wide in twin silent screams.

And then I'd wake, again and again, each waking a continuation of the nightmare. I'd remember in those first pellucid seconds, that Persephone (at my urging!) had taken a blade and some unspeakable skill to my gills, cutting, weaving, stitching, and chanting through the purple-green dusk and into the star rashed night, until I had been utterly changed.

Until I could breathe sky-side air.

But something had been lost. My vocal chords had been severed in the...procedure. There is always a price. I know that now. And I know something else: Persephone does not grant wishes. She grants curses. For I had only desired, she told me later, her voice effervescent with triumph, to be able to seek and live in the human world. For which, she told me, I required merely the ability to breath air. Not necessarily, she chuckled, the ability to walk on two legs. I had not specified that particular caveat.

For there were plenty of animals on the land like me, she said. That slither and grovel on their bellies.

Chapter 7

When I was a child, my sisters and I would explore the fantastical vastness of the Coral Keep in games of hide and seek that would last from sunrise to dusk. There were – are – tunnels that spin and wind, eel-like, beneath the fortress, seemingly endless. They burrow under the sea bed like thirsting veins. Amonie was fearful of these and could be dragged along only with great reluctance, but Sephona, Clista, Kelan and I loved to try to lose ourselves, and each other, within their thick-walled coils.

When we were very young – just twenty years old or so, Clista and I, barely out of clouts, enjoyed nothing more than seeking, throughout the Keep's many passages and turrets and slopes, the mosaics and etchings that were made by our mother. We would trace their patterns and ridges with our small fingers, imagining that, instead of shale and shell, our fingertips were caressing the lines of her face, the small bones of her wrists, the delicate ridge-like webbing of her adipose fin. They were our only way to know her. All we had of her.

In later years, Clista, of the golden hair and the sweet tones that made her an easy favourite with Father, loved dearly to collect the minerals that could be eased from the walls and floors of the mid-chambers, which hung a fathom or more beneath the bulk of the Keep itself. Into her weed-spun bag went shards of aragonite, chunks of peridotite, and spotted serpentine. Sephona desired, even then, to drape herself in decorations made of such, but did not deign to fashion such ornamentation with her own hands. Instead, Seph would bide her time, watching as Clista, in the night-time dim of their shared chamber, wove the gems onto strands of finest half-plastic – manufactured here by the folk – creating necklaces and hairnets and tail dazzlers of such beauty that they soon became one of the wonders of the Realm. And, Sephona whispered to our golden sister, who, really, was best placed to do justice to such treasures? Because, surely, Clista was fair to look upon; and, naturally, Amonie's sweet natured modesty was appealing; and, of course, Kelan's diplomacy and skills in statecraft marked her as a natural successor to our father.

Contemplating me, Sephona merely looked amused and, tossing her black hair into a thick fragrant swirl, declared that she, herself, possessed all the attributes of her sisters combined. And then she laughed, as if it was all in fun, and disappearing beyond the mid-chambers into the passages that wound yet deeper into the rock, called back for us to catch her. Laughing too, we did. But later, she wore Clista's beautiful creations and, it is true, looked like a queen. Maybe even a goddess, as she sparkled, high headed, through the upper towers and state rooms of the Keep.

It was only my family, and a few carefully chosen attendants, who had the freedom of the Keep. It has always been thus. We are not royalty, but my father's prerogatives are such that it makes no difference. In times of crisis, though, a number of the Great Halls have been opened for the folk to shelter within. In my life-time, this has only happened once, during a monstrous storm that permeated the ocean's layers. It pulled the cordons in brutal tugs that kept the mesh as razor wire for the rise and fall of two moons, and destroyed more than half of our functioning bivalve farms. I remember the masses sheltering within our walls, Grandmother regally circulating, and the staff, ragged gilled, as they struggled to feed thousands from the stored provisions. Sephona allowed herself to be seen a couple of times, and Amonie had to be restrained from her continuous efforts to assist those distressed by the displacement.

It passed, surely enough, the crisis. Just another storm my father weathered, another rip-tide whose passage he seemingly subverted with the sheer force of his will. Much like the rebellion.

One day, some moons after this, and still well before any of us, my sisters and I, came of age at our half century year, Sephona became seriously ill. With shocking suddenness, she weakened and sickened; her breath became labored, and a foul stink emanated from her gills as if a pestilence festered and raged deep within her. None of us had ever seen its like, and the Elders were summoned.

Grandmother tended her day and night, leaving her side to neither eat nor sleep, preferring to doze by Sephona's bed and have all her meals delivered to where she stayed sentinel. Yet still, my sister deteriorated. Her fins stiffened, her scales peeled off in nauseating sheaves, and her tail spasmed in horrific pulses. Often, she could not be roused from a shallowed, fevered sleep.

We prepared for the worst. Father was stonily desperate as healers from the Hub came and went without a diagnosis. Without a cure. My sisters and I wrung our hands outside the sick room and the Realm prepared to mourn.

And then, one sunrise, we woke to find Sephona gone. I do not mean expired. I mean *gone*. In the literal sense of the word. Grandmother, waking from her usual fitful sleep, claimed to have seen and heard nothing. When she had drifted into a semi dreaming state sometime after the quarter moon began its slow slide from the sky's summit, Sephona had been curled in her bed, only partly lucid, stinking of half rotted meat. But now she was gone. Vanished.

Father, once told, also disappeared, and could not be found.

The Keep became frantic. Grandmother, in Father's absence, summoned the Sirens. The very guts of the Keep were searched and probed, as our warriors sent sonar pulses through rock and passageway until they were satisfied that no being, living or dead, hid in the most secret and intimate spaces of our great fortress.

During this time, Amonie and Clista could not be induced to leave their rooms. Kelan confined herself to the minor chambers of state, in conference with ministers and members of Father's trusted retinue. And I shadowed the Sirens, following them into tunnels buried deep below the Keep. So deep in places, that the darkness was totally unalleviated, and the passageways so tight that, one time, my tail near jammed and, panic crazed, I had to thrash my way clear. After which, I was ordered to return to my chambers.

My Grandmother, looking much nearer her three hundredth year than she was, seemed on the verge of making an announcement to the realm when, three sun births and sun deaths after her disappearance, Sephona returned to us. Cured. She appeared in the gardens, near to the shaded walls where my red flower would one day take root. I was the first to sight her.

I rushed to my sister, frantic with relief.

She would not tell me where she had been or what had transpired there, but just kept her eyes calmly fixed on mine, even as I shook her shoulders and shouted questions into her face. The scales of Sephona's tail were once more gold and pink tinged, iridescent in the early morning light; her skin glowed silver in its vitality, and even her hair appeared more lustrous, billowing in a cloud that immersed my own like a fragrant lake of ink.

"What has happened to you, Sephona?" I persisted. "Where have you been? Father is gone, also, seeking for you, no doubt…"

And it was then that I realized there was something different about her. It was her eyes. They were the shimmering green of sea moss kissed by the slanted light of a summer sunset, where before they had been storm grey. These eyes sparkled and glittered with something I did not recognize as belonging to my elder sister.

"Sephona," I whispered. "Your eyes."

I dropped my hands from her shoulders, letting the gentle current nudge my arms beside me in the water.

My sister raised a hand, unthinkingly, to her face, but allowed it to fall away before it made a connection with her skin.

"I was sick," she said, and her voice, at least, was as condescending as I remembered it. "But now I am well. Now I am strong."

"Father must be told you are returned…" I began.

"He is with the Magister," she interrupted.

"Grandmother must be summoned," I started.

Once more Sephona's voice cut between my words, a dorsal fin through water. "She is with Father at this very moment. Listen, sister. I have been most marvelously healed. Rejoice, merely. So effective has this well-making been that, truly, I am more complete than I was before I sickened. It is a wondrous thing. Be happy."

"Who healed you, Sephona? Where have you been?"

"The Hub, of course. Where else?"

My gills gaped wide at the blatancy of the lie, and oxygen flooded by lungs. The Sirens had searched the Hub in its entirely, firing sonar into its most secret spaces. I had been with them.

"And Father?" I breathed.

"With me."

"Sephona…"

"Do hush, sister. You know, I am most alarmingly hungry. Go tell the kitchen staff to prepare something, will you? Dulse and sea cradle…yes. That is what I must have. Do you mind? And then gather our sisters. I want to hear all the gossip that I have missed in my confinement. Has Torfel began courting Maina? And what of Aglaope? Grandmother said, before I fell ill, that she was set to begin her trials? And Clista: has she fashioned something beautiful for me, in her sorrow? Oh, never mind; just go summon them."

I swam away in a daze.

My sisters, shortly after I broke the news to them, clustered in a pack around Sephona, wondering, questioning, touching her face, her hair, the near luminescent silver-blue of her arms and belly. Yet they elicited no more answers than I had. The same reticence was true of Father who was, indeed, to be found cloistered with the Magister and both his Great and Small Councils. He could not be induced to furnish us with any details of Sephona's disappearance, his own vanishing, or Seph's sudden reappearance, cured of blight and with newly shaded eyes. He remained tight lipped, simply stating, as Sephona had, that they had been guests of The Hub.

The Realm was furnished with a story. It went thus: Father and Sephona had retreated to a sacred cavern buried so far within the bowels of The Hub as to be almost completely inaccessible. Brutal tidal swells made the single passage to its innards passable for a single moon shift once every season. The rare minerals found in the cave (so it was stated in an official proclamation) permeated the water and had such efficacious healing powers – when combined with certain secret practices of the First Elder – that they had brought about Seph's complete recovery and subsequent return to the Realm.

The folk rejoiced. My sisters were curious, suspicious even, but had been made malleable with the combined strains of grief and relief. And Grandmother? She watched it all unfold, her lips stretched in a tight smile that, at times, looked to be bearing such weight that it seemed to be the only thing keeping the expression on her face in place. Ensuring that it didn't change into...something else.

It was only later, much later, quivering with fever and pain on a flat rock in my own healing cave, gills torn out and each breath like pulling fire into my lungs and expelling hot ash, that it finally dawned on me who, exactly, had cured Sephona. I remembered how it had been my sister who had given me the key to Persephone's cell. How Seph had urged me…goaded me, even, into opening that prison door. I began, then, to understand what the price of the cure had been. And who had paid it.

Chapter 8

We have arrived at my present. The Realm, the witch, the knife, the flat-topped rock…my family. They are all past now, and it is as if I can see each of these elements of my story, but from a great distance. A distance that is growing with every second that I lie, beached, on this dust-dry sand, the sun above, unfiltered by wave and water, a focused ball of fire that is slowly roasting the scales of my tail. I know that if I do not find shade, I will perish here. It is not, necessarily, an unwelcome thought.

My small bag of woven sea grass is crushed beneath my belly; its contents are all I have from home. I can only imagine the desperation with which Grandmother and my sisters will be seeking me at this very moment. The resigned disappointment which he has, no doubt, long expected, with which Father will summon the Sirens, believing me to have fled beyond the cordons in a fit of rebellious rage. He will feel sure that I shall be found, quivering and lost, to be brought gratefully back to the fold to begin a lengthy spell in my tower suite. Considering this, my resolve strengthens, and I turn my head away from the sea, looking in the other direction towards the scrubby foliage that fringes the beach.

With a tremendous effort, I move one arm forward, and then the other, dragging myself along the sand. My arm muscles are not used to moving in this way. The lack of resistance to the movement is countered by the effort required to haul the weight of my body without the aid of the water, and I find my limbs flailing clumsily. I cannot believe my own mass. I feel bulky, gargantuan, like a whale that has floundered into shallow waters and become stranded on a flat.

By the time I reach the shelter of the low and ragged trees, the sun has sunk from the sky's peak and hovers, ferocious, in the midpoint of the heavens. I am sweat caked and sand-blown. My pelvic fins are a pair of dried out tatters emerging from the flesh of my lower stomach. My adipose fin, trailing from the small of my back, is surely blistered in the heat. I dare not heave my body over to inspect myself, for fear of what I will see. My tail is the worst, as it throbs in the dry air, scales and soft flesh beneath contracting and splitting in the searing glare of the day's malevolent eye. I close my own eyes, briefly, and will the falling of the night. It does not help.

After some unknown time, I roll onto my side. The tide stretched sea has become a distant shimmer of blue-yellow, and I imagine how it would feel to be submerged within its cool and salted embrace. The phantom feelings this invokes are so visceral that, for a few seconds, my skin and scales tingle with the conjured sensation. I shake away the thought and push myself up into a sitting position, though it takes three attempts. Twice my arms refuse to support the weight of my torso and I crash back, without grace, onto the sand. But on the third try, I lunge my body forward as I lever myself up, and the momentum pitches me upright. I steady myself, just before toppling over (this time face first), and balance in a sitting position, tail outstretched in front of me, one finger-stretched palm holding me steady.

I use my free hand to unlace the many beaded ties of my bag, pulling out a whelk shell that has been stuffed with kelp butter and sealed with a tapered pebble. I smear the unguent over my tail and fins, the relief instant and blissful. A greasy layer remains on the top layers of the flesh and scales to which it has been applied, which I know will make the following few hours bearable. Next from the bag, I take the sectosteroid pills, wrapped in half-plastic, that

Persephone gave me before bringing me here. She told me to swallow one each morning to prevent infection, following the...surgery. I choke one down, then let myself fall back onto the beach once more. Exhaustion overtakes me completely and, before I even realise that I have closed my eyes, I am asleep and dreaming.

***

When I come to, it is full dark, and the forest in whose shadow I slept is alive with sound and secret movement. The moon is a smooth white sea urchin that rides the night's swell and the sound of the ocean, creeping up the ridges of the beach once more, soothes me profoundly. I feel a trickle of renewed strength, and push myself up, a little easier this time.

I consider my options. I cannot return to the Realm, even if I did desire to do so. I no longer have the capacity, physically, to live among the folk. True, I could throw myself into the sea now, swim to the borders and beg their mercy. Seeing my condition, my father may deign to allow me to live out my life in a secluded air pocketed cave beyond the cordons; perhaps the one that Persephone's mother had the pleasure of. I do not think that he would create an air-fed cell in The Pit for me…but I cannot be sure. Who knows what havoc Persephone has wreaked since I last saw her two tides ago? I made her swear, as part of the services she rendered me, that she would not seek to harm the folk or revenge herself on my family. At the time, I believed her. I think I still do.

I cannot live a semi-life on the outskirts of the ocean. I have no shelter, limited means to feed myself, and I do not know how to access the fresh water that I now must take into myself. Before leaving me here, Persephone held a small flask to my lips and tipped liquid into my mouth. There was no longer the spongy flesh at the back of my throat to prevent its passage into my innards. Terrified at the sensation, I gagged and retched until the whole lot came back up to spatter onto the sand.

"Once more," Persephone had said. "Relax your throat this time."

The same thing happened again. And again.

I couldn't speak it, but Persephone must have seen the near-enraged "I can't!" in my eyes.

She bent so that her blue eyes looked straight into mine. "You can. You must. You need this now. Thirst is something you will never feel, yet you must seek out fresh water every day, and drink of it, or you will die. Do you understand?"

Eventually, I was able to suppress my panic and allow the water to pass down my throat and into my body. Satisfied, Persephone put a second flask, full and tightly stoppered, into my woven bag, and pulled its strings tight.

When she left, she did not say goodbye.

Now, gazing at the clear and unwavering splash of stars above me, I consider the last of my options: to seek out the human habitation that Persephone has assured me lies close by, due east of this beach, and….and…see what comes of it. I cannot allow myself to think too closely about the possible consequences of this course of action or about the details of the low-crawling journey that it will necessitate. Instead, I allow myself to drift in a contemplation of the wonders that will be revealed to me once I have arrived. Of the soul that I will seek and, dearly hope, will receive as my own. Of how, in possession of such, I will know no death; I will not dissolve in my third century, my dreams half formed and my destiny a near-blank map.

I am roused from these thoughts by a great noise, far out to sea. A boat is there, a huge three masted vessel, larger than the biggest that I have seen, half buried and just visible beyond the edges of the

Realm's northern cordons. The noise is an explosion, as sudden and loud as the odd seasonal thermal detonations from the sea-bed vents. A moment after the crackle-boom, a white flower of fire blooms in the sky above the ship, its petals peeling off to fall towards the ocean in diminishing sparks that trail creamy embers.

I can only stare, silent and open mouthed. The far off, tiny sound of screaming drifts land-wards. Even at this distance, I can tell the ship is listing, and that it is cutting a stumbling, pitching path through the gentle waves. I do not think it will make it safely to the shore.

I am overtaken by a certainty that I know so utterly to be true that I gasp with the knowledge. The ship has been wrecked. But something has gone awry. The Wreckers, for some unknowable reason, have not been able to cleanly snare their prey, and it has limped away before the Sirens have seen to the wholesale slaughter of its crew. I see in my mind the human creature that Father killed, and I feel, once more, the warm wash of his blood on my face. I must try to save those on the drowning ship. I am almost certain that I will die in the attempt, but the risk seems, to me, a fair one. As Persephone told me, a life is owed for a life that is taken. I am not my father, to be sure, but maybe I can repay part of the debt in his name.

Leaving my woven bag, I pull myself back down the beach towards the water. The sand, dampened and cooled by the night's moist breath is smoother, and I am able to swiftly slither the shortened distance to the waves. The sea water, as it splashes up first around my neck and face, making me cough, lifts the weight of my body in its embrace. It is overwhelming, and I raise my face to the moon in a silent howl of pleasure and sorrow as it bears me from the land.

I swim hard, keeping my head above water and ignoring my body's physical imperative to dive deep and arrow to my destination, to arch and slide through the currents. Instead, I keep my sight on the foundering craft and push through the water, thrashing my tail as fast as I am able. My fins drag out behind me uselessly, utterly unsuitable for this mode of swimming. I make a brief attempt to hold my breath and duck beneath the waves, the commands of my body becoming too strong to ignore. My newly fashioned gills and lungs, however, will have none of it: after a mere couple of seconds, my chest is on fire and the agony is so great, I am forced to return to the surface of the water and expel the captured air from my body.

The distance to the boat narrows until I am approaching its tilted hull. As I near, another explosion fills the night, and my head darts up to see a fire has ignited on the deck. There are more screams and moans, and my heart quails at what I will find. And what I can do. An almighty crunching-cracking sound comes from deep within the guts of the vessel, as it splits in two. A pair of human forms fall through the newly made chasm to crash into the wreckage-strewn water just a few strokes from me. Sporadic fires flicker among the now floating cargo and spars of wood, and a conflagration gobbles at the remainder of the boat as it slowly pitches into the deep.

I am frozen in place, tail undulating below the waves in a slow rhythm, my mind shocked to blankness, when the shouts of one of the humans who had fallen into the water permeates my horror, and I swim to him. He is pulling at the companion who had fallen with him, shrieking what, I think, must have been the man's name. This man is clearly dead, a thick, jagged spear of timber jutting from his stomach, free flowing blood streaming from an injury to his skull.

I touch the shouting human on the shoulder. He turns, eyes crazed and unseeing, and tries to strike at me, never letting go of his dead fellow. I see that he has sustained a grievous wound to his arm, where the bone protrudes in a moon-silvered spike.

Instinctively, I try to speak to him, but, of course, no words emerge. Instead, I attempt once more to take hold of his arm, to pull him toward the far-off land. This time, I am able to pull his body towards me as easily as a clump of sea lettuce, and I realize he has fainted.

Gently, I detach his knuckle-white grip on his dead companion and haul him towards the shore.

Severance

Chapter 9

A shoal of skiffs sprints through the water, making for the bloody, burning wreckage out at sea. Voices shout frantically from aboard a number of the crafts, and I feel nauseating pulses of adrenaline polluting the air and sea around me, making it hard to think clearly, to act with conviction. I try to signal them, but my frantic splashing and beating of the water with the palm of my free hand goes unnoticed in the froth and wash of their passage. The people on these boats shout – I hear them distantly – as they draw nearer to the floating carnage of the dead ship, seeking survivors.

At last, I haul my living cargo onto the sand and lie there a moment, my body half submerging the form of the man beneath me, panting roughly and heart beating a sharp rhythm in my chest. Rolling onto my side, I look at this human creature I have dragged from the deep. He seems to be wholly indistinguishable from the man Father killed, from the dead creature in the water, companion to this one. From the other human leaves that fell in a silent shower around me after I watched the Sirens bring down their ship, so many moons ago. Perhaps this is merely a matter of refining my perceptions.

I touch, softly, his strangely coloured peach-brown skin, warm beneath my fingers. I wonder about the mysteries he and his kind can reveal to me.

Blood is still trickling from the terrible wound in his arm, and I press my palm tentatively against the flow, applying pressure. His eyes flutter open and he looks straight at me. His eyes take in my skin, my fins, my tail. Seized with fear, he shuffles back through the sand on his elbows, eyes wide and fevered. He believes me to be a Siren.

I open my mouth to reassure him, forgetting my severed voice.

I notice one of his hands scrabbling in the shale, but I do not understand the meaning of the action until it is too late. The small, jagged edged rock smashes into my temple and the world becomes a night with no stars, no moon, nothing.

***

Voices. Legs. The weird rounded shapes of bent knees. Flower patterned material spread out on the sand. The sound of the sea a limitless caress in the near distance. I sit bolt upright…or try to, but find my arms are tied together at the wrist and offer no leverage. I am forced to remain on my back, rigid.

A group of humans is gathered around me. Some stand, others have folded their legs beneath them to crouch on the beach; all flinch backwards at

121

my sudden movement, their mouths forming little 'o's. I point to a human at random and then begin patting at the sand beside me, attempting to communicate the idea of the man I pulled from the doomed ship. Murmurs ripple through the small crowd like the pulse of a jellyfish's tentacles:

"It is trying to speak with us!"

"Has it a voice?"

"What does it want?"

"It is an abomination!"

"She means Christian…"

"It was her that pulled him from the sea…"

I point to the woman who said this last and nod my head. She is one of the kneelers, and she leans in closer to me. Her hair is hidden by a cap, her face lined with deep grooves, but her eyes are kind. She reaches out a nervous hand to my face.

A voice from the crowd admonishes: "Bethel! Have a care; it may bite!"

"Give over," the woman says, her eyes not leaving mine. Her fingers touch my hair, and she strokes the dried-out strands of it back from my brow and cheeks with a firm hand. Grandmother once told us, in a story, that the Old Ones would leak water from their eyes when overcome with a strong emotion. She said that, for us, it would have been akin to losing air bubbles from our eyelids when we felt particularly happy or sad. I remember that Amonie, particularly, used to laugh at this, until Grandmother threatened to wind up the tale early and dispatch us to bed before our time. I recall this now and think that, maybe, I can finally understand the relief that tears must bring when the physical package of your form feels too small to contain the mixed tidal surges of sorrow and joy.

"Bethel…"

The woman ignores the warning voice. Her eyes remain fixed on my face.

"You want to know of Christian, don't you? It was you pulled him from the wreck, wasn't it? Saved his life, no doubt. Not that he has repaid you well..." Her fingers move to the side of my head and she presses, with the lightest of touches, the blood clotted wound there. I wince.

"Easy now," she continues. "He gave you a nasty knock there. We'll get that cleaned up for you." She stands and addresses the others: "Make up a litter. Carry her to the Temple and round up any novices you can find. Tell them to heat salted water and prepare clean linens."

Another woman's voice: "Is this wise, Bethel? Should we not simply cast her back into the depths from which she came?" A muted flurry of polite agreement.

"Don't be such a fool," the woman called Bethel snaps back. She takes her hand from my head and stands. "And untie her at once." She begins to turn away but then, at the last minute, kneels close to me in the sand again. "And Christian. The man you saved. He does well. His arm has been reset and splinted, and his life is in no danger. Thanks to you."

I smile at her, and her face becomes, in its surprise, a blank oval. Slowly, she smiles back at me, and it is the sweetest thing I have ever experienced in my life.

She leaves, followed by a few members of the gathered huddle, disappearing beneath the trees in a path that must run through the forest. One of the remaining male humans kneels from his standing position near my head, and brings a knife to bear, swiftly, on the cords capturing my wrists. The flax breaks with a brittle snap. A woman helps me rise to a sitting position, though I sense her unwillingness to touch my skin in the tenseness of her hands and in the fear pheromones that are rising from her in waves. I catch her fingers with my own and point to a nearby spot where my woven bag lies abandoned. I make a looping gesture around my neck and point again. The woman follows, with her eyes, to the spot I have indicated, and rises, walking the few steps to where my bag nestles, wretched, in the sand.

"This?" she asks.

I shape the word "yes" with my lips and hold out my hands.

"Wait," says a voice from behind my head. The woman looks a question at the voice's owner. "Give it here."

I watch as the woman passes the bag over my head to the waiting hands. Outraged, I make a grab for it but, unaccustomed still to moving on the land, I succeed only in mis-balancing and flopping onto my back on the sand. There is a short laugh that is cut off abruptly. As I am struggling to wrench myself upright again, my belongings are dropped, one by one, around me. The flask of water is opened and tossed down to trickle out its precious fresh water on the beach; the kelp butter shoveled from its shell and flicked to the ground; the painted pebble that was Amonie's. The souls, however, do not fall.

There is a short, breathy silence.

The man who has taken my bag leans close to my ear. I still cannot see his face but his voice is a hiss: "Where did you get these?"

I cannot think how to mime the long-ago ship-wreck, my failed attempt to save the sailor doomed by Father's obsidian knife. I try to turn my face to speak to my questioner, but at my slight movement, he darts out a hand that encircles my throat in an iron grip. His fingers press against the half-healed wound in my neck and I shriek silently, my tail thrashing involuntarily against the hard-packed sand.

"Janka! For God's sake!"

A couple of the other onlookers move to intervene, but as suddenly as they had appeared at my throat, the man's hands vanish, and I hear him stand and move back a couple of quick paces. At the same moment, there is movement on the wooded path, and I see two of the people who had left with Bethel returning, carrying a flimsy looking wood and fabric contraption between them.

Wordlessly, they approach and lay the thing down on the sand next to me. A man and the woman who had passed me my bag put their hands on my shoulders and the thick shaft of my tail and shuffle me onto the material that is now stretched rigid beside me. Realising what is happening, I lean over, scrabbling in the sand for Amonie's pebble and trying to scoop up as much of the kelp butter as I am able to. Someone passes me the pebble but before I can retrieve more than a finger-tip's worth of butter, the man called Janka steps forward and crushes it into the ground with the strangely formed appendages on the end of his legs that I know, from Grandmother's tales, are called feet.

I act without thinking. I curl my fingers into a fist around Amonie's beautiful stone and hurl it at Janka. It connects with his head, just above the ear. In the moment before he lunges at me, a silence falls that is so profound that even the pull and wash of the sea fades and is lost entirely. There is just the beat of my heart, slow and sure, in my ears, and pulsing in the tender flesh of my neck.

And then Janka is on me, tearing and spitting, foam from his open mouth dripping onto my face. His nails rake one moment at the scales of my tail, the next burrowing through my hair, seeking the skin of my scalp. The others try to pull him off, but his rage-driven strength is such that he clings to me like a barnacle. My arms are crushed beneath him and I can only beat at him with my tail. He is impervious to the blows, though, and I am sure he will kill me when, suddenly, he becomes limp and rolls off and away from me with a groan, a hand to the back of his head.

Bethel stands above me, a staff in her hand. Pink blood and a few strands of hair coat its tip.

She points it at Janka: "Take him to the Jury House." Two men haul Janka up by the elbows and half drag him away, leaving the beach and following the path through the forest.

The old woman passes her staff to the female human who had brought my bag and bends to take the front poles that are connected to the material on which I still lay. Another lifts the rear poles and suddenly I am air-borne. As I am carried through the trees, their wondrous limbs and leaves casting pond-like shadows on my body and those of my fellows, a hand reaches out to pass me Amonie's painted pebble, retrieved from where it fell on the beach.

When I bring it closer to my face, I see how the delicate depiction of the green coral tower of the Keep's east wing is now stained with the rusty crimson of a human's blood.

Severance

Chapter 10

I am taken to a sprawling white building that I later learn is called a church. In a way that I cannot fathom, it seems that the humans' souls come here for sustenance and rest, sometimes with their hosts, sometimes without. The church nestles in a grove of orange and lemon trees, and the brightness of the fruit combined with the dry glare of the building's walls is still a wonder to me.

Many moons have risen and fallen since I came here – I have watched them from the window of my chamber – and here I have remained, seeing the occasional visitor and being tended by the novices whose kindnesses, great and small, have made a miracle of my experience of humanity, whatever else may have come before or is yet to unfold. Of Janka, there has been no sight and, of course, I am glad of it.

The novices and I have developed a type of sign language and can now communicate fairly effectively – if haltingly. I have been able to indicate the agony inducing dryness of my scales and fins and, while I was unable to convey 'kelp butter', they understood what was required well enough to make up a decent substitute with a form of oil and crushed herbs. This concoction brings me a relief almost as great as the kelp butter. The novices also clean and tend the now fast healing wounds on my neck. I think they understand what has happened to me, but they quail when I try to sign the details and, after many attempts, I have finally given up on it.

Bethel comes daily. I think she holds some power here, but its derivation or purpose I have not discovered. Bethel does understand my situation. Not the how's or the who's or the why's of it, but she knows I have chosen to be changed and to come among human-kind. She seems bewildered by it. She tells me that, when I am fully recovered, I shall have a pair of crutches made so that, with practice, I may navigate this new world by myself. That, if I wish it, I could have a dress fashioned that would cover my tail and fins. Although, she says, laughing, as there's nothing to hide my silvery skin, perhaps a gown is not really the best thing, after all.

The novices bring me fresh water and food a few times a day. They offer me cooked trout and donkey-shrimp. When I first tasted such food, cooked as it was, I couldn't help but spit the mouthful I'd taken straight back out. I can tolerate such meals better, now, though, and my ministers have also learned to bring me cool stews of algae and sea nettle and dulse which they know I love and which better agrees with my constitution.

I marvel most, though, at the exotic, wondrous softness of human beds. And I still wonder at how one can settle into such luxurious warmth without the need to half cocoon oneself into bed to prevent drifting to the bedchamber's ceiling.

Christian – that is the name of the man I pulled from the water – visits me, too.

He is fascinated by my skin, more than my useless tail and fins, and I know he likes to touch it; I see it in his eyes. The humans' skin is warm, their hearts heat it, deep within themselves. This warmth is startling to the touch. My own blood is different. It runs cool in my arteries and no exertion will excite it to the simmer that those now around me experience when they run or swim or dance. When Christian first came to see me, he laid a hand on my arm, and immediately recoiled, as surprised, I think, by its lack of warmth as by its smooth, silver-blue iridescence.

I must confess, at his touch, I believe my heart would have agitated the blood in my veins to a low heat if it were able.

I begin to see, now, the many differences in the faces and bodies of the human creatures. They are each as unique as conch shells that have been warped and caressed by the turning of many tides. Grandmother's tales held a number of truths, it appears: I have learnt that these people really do live only a fraction of years compared to the life spans of the folk. Yet, as the novice named Anna likes to tell me, human souls live on for eternity. There are many souls here. All the novices wear great metal souls around their necks, and Bethel and Christian both bear smaller ones on chains around their own. In my room, there are a number of painted souls: I imagine that they must have belonged to esteemed leaders of this particular tribe.

I remember Persephone's words to me, spoken as we lingered in the 'healing' cave before I was delivered here: "Should you earn the love of a human, he or she will share their soul with you freely. And then you will never die, never dissolve into water and flesh and foam, but instead will follow your human into the worlds that follow this one. An unlikely scenario, Dearest; but who am I to judge?"

The third time he came, Christian saw me looking at his soul, and he held up the chain it hung from, moving closer towards where I lay so that I could see it.

"This?" he asked. "You like this?"

I reached out my fingers, moving them over the polished wood of the small twin bars.

"Janka said you had some like it…" he trailed off.

I tried to sign, in the rudimentary language the novices and I have developed, that Janka had taken them from me on the beach. In my anger, I rose to a half sitting position in the bed. My tail, beneath its burden of heavy sheets, thrashed once, twice. I saw Christian look at the shape of it, so strange to him, and the distaste that curled his lip before he could hide it. He put a hand to my shoulder and eased me back to my pillows.

"Easy now, it's okay. Janka took the crucifixes from you; is that right?"

Crucifixes. That must be the name they give their souls when they are leashed.

I signed an affirmative.

Christian sighed and walked the few paces from my bed to the window that looked out onto the startling brightness of the orange grove.

"Where did you get them?" he asked me, without turning. "Did you find them?"

He came to sit at my bedside once more.

"Did you take them from a human? Have you met with humans before?"

I looked at him, unsure of how to respond. Before I had time to frame a clumsy answer with my hands, he went on: "We have heard of your people, you know. As a little boy, at my mother's knee, I was told the stories of the folk that went into the sea, after the Ravage. Of our kin in the water, that hide in the deep and have adapted totally to live beneath the waves. I was told, as was my father and his father before him, that the division of our species was unnatural, caused by the radiation rather than being an evolutionary response to it." He paused. "In the tales, your kind bring poison and corruption to mine."

He looked at me, taking in the horror and sorrow on my face.

"We only half believed it, generation to generation," he went on. "What started long ago as truth, it turns out, became half fairytale, half myth.

And then you washed up onto the shore. Or rather, I washed up onto the shore, thanks to you."

He tried for a smile, but it was lopsided, and something I could not name lurked within it.

"Will you take me to your kin?"

And it was then that one of the lined and stooped novices (elderly – at just ninety!) bustled into the room carrying a tray of fresh bandages and poultice. Christian hastily looked away from me and got to his feet, as if he had not asked the question at all. He wished me a polite farewell and left. And that was the last time I saw him.

How strange, to find I miss his company, when I have had the pleasure of so little of it.

It nears dusk again now, and the faint, low tumble and crash of the sea is a constant comfort and torment to me. Every night, I dream of the Realm, and of my sisters tight within it. It is these dreams that I am just slipping into when the creak of my chamber door opening pulls me back to the solid, dry ground of my new reality.

It is Janka. He stands in the doorway, a grey shadow, watching me without words. I sit upright and reach out my hand for the bell on the bedside table that the novices have left for me in order to summon them if I need assistance. As fast as the turning swirl of a cloud of pig krill, Janka is at my side, his hand gripping my wrist before my fingers can curl round the bell. He leans close to me, as Christian did so that I could study his soul. But Janka's breath is sour, and his mouth spits words at me with undisguised hatred.

"I know where you got the chains," he hisses at me. "I am not enchantment blinded like these other fools, looking at you all doe-eyed as if you've stepped straight from a story of make believe. You killed for them, didn't you? You have seen our kind before, and you've pulled them down into the deep. We've had boats disappear over the years. Always been that way. These dullards I live amongst blame storms or mechanics or there being too much grog aboard. But I think I know different, since you dragged your wretchedness onto our shores."

Janka pulls from his shirt one of the chained souls he had stolen from me.

"You see this one?" he says. I try again to pull my wrist free, but he has it fast. "Belonged to my brother."

He lifts his free hand then, and I think he means to strike me, but instead he merely points a finger at me and, releasing my arm, backs out of the room, his eyes not leaving mine.

When he has gone, a great despair washes over me. For how can I ever explain to them – Janka, Christian, all of them – the nature of the Realm and the truths that I have learned? Of the falsity of the cordons; of the Sirens; of the ignorance in which the folk have been kept? Of the Wreckers? That the souls I have did, indeed, come from the bodies of their lost kin?

The moon is floating high in the sky when eventually I sleep. My dreams are troubled and strange. My sisters come to me, one after the other, begging me to return to them. My grandmother wrings her ringed hands and wails, her voice rising like mist from beneath the waves. And Persephone. She slinks into my sleeping mind, smiling and sweet faced, to offer me a coral knife. It lays on her outstretched palms like something new born.

"This is for Christian," she says. "Put it into his heart as he lays sleeping. Do this for the protection of the folk, lest your kin be slaughtered. For you will lead them to the Realm, whether you desire it or no. You will lead them to your family." She smiles wider, so that I think her lips will split.

"And when you feel his blood flow out and over your fingers, and his skin turns cool, like yours, put your hand to his cheek and look into his eyes and tell him that humanity's debt is repaid."

Severance

Chapter 11

The next morning, I wait for Christian. He usually comes on this day. The novices have given me a stone and chalk tablet and told me the names of the days and hours. They roll around like the tides, in a never-ending loop. So I know that I can expect him soon. I have made up my mind to explain it all to him, as well as I am able. Everything. The Wreckers, Persephone, the whole of it.

But instead of Christian, Bethel puts her head around the door, smiling a greeting at me before entering the room. She has brought me fresh flowers from her garden and I take them, delighted, putting them to my nose to breath in their near overwhelming fragrance. She puts them in a jar for me, fussing over them and murmuring about the weather and the stillness of the ocean. I realise she has something she wishes to tell me.

Gently, I catch her arm, and look a question at her.

Bethel sighs and, leaving the flowers, sits next to me. I am feeling much stronger this morning, and Anna has propped up my pillows so that I can easily sit upright.

I make the sign for "Christian."

Bethel sighs again.

"Is he unwell?" I sign.

Bethel leans forward in her chair, her elbows on her knees.

"You must know," she begins. She pauses for a moment, and then continues. "I can see it on your face. Your feelings for Christian."

I make a flurry of embarrassed hand gestures but, seeing Bethel's look, give it up.

"Hear me," Bethel says. "Christian is to wed another. You understand this word, 'wed'? He is to be bonded to another.

"Besides, Child," she strokes my hair, "you could never have paired. It would not have been permitted. You must quash these feelings down, deep within yourself. In time, they will fade, like a barely remembered dream."

My companion becomes brisk. Taking a small piece of fabric from her sleeve, she wipes at my face (my cheeks are wet! Even through the veil of my embarrassment, I am amazed: I had not thought the folk could cry), and stands. "Enough of that," she snaps, not without kindness. "I have something for you." Bethel leaves the room, returning with a pair of stout wooden poles, rounded on one end and curved at the other.

"Crutches," Bethel says. "I think the time is coming when you're going to be able to use them."

I thank her heartily, with hands and eyes. She leaves soon after, sensing, no doubt, that I need to nurse my own foolishness in privacy. I hope, despite what Bethel has told me, that Christian will come again to visit me. At the same time, I am mortified at the thought that he will. I resolve, when Bethel comes again, to tell her my tale in full instead, and trust to her judgement on the consequences of such an action. I will tell her, too, of Janka's appearance in my room last night, and of the words he spoke to me.

The morning draws out and dies. I eat a noon meal and sleep a little. There are no dreams. I wake in the late afternoon, the air that puffs in from my window smelling aged and dusty. I look at the crutches in the corner and think of the sea. It rumbles and churns just a short distance down the forest path from here.

Perhaps because I am not thinking entirely clearly, I lower myself from the bed and pull myself across the floor of my room to where the crutches are propped against the wall. My tail drags across the floor, leaving a glistening trail of scented oil. I pull the poles down to me and try to use them to lever my body upright. Three times I tumble to the ground, the crutches falling atop me. Each time, I listen for the sound of one or more of the novices hurrying along the corridor to see what has happened. It remains quiet. The church's residents, I know, take their souls to a gathering in the chapel at this hour, and they sing to them.

Finally, I manage to maneuver myself into a 'standing' position. I realise that the curved tops of the crutches are handholds, and I use these tentatively, putting my weight onto one pole, and then the other, my tail swinging beneath them. It creates a terrible drag where, in the water, it allowed me to dart and arrow with slippery speed. Very slowly, I use the crutches to haul myself out of my room and down the bare corridor. Just ahead, a small archway marks the entrance to the gardens and, beyond, the outside world. I trudge on, one pole forward, then the next. I think of the ocean, determined to reach it.

I pass beneath the archway. I traverse the gardens where the flowers are a mosaic in a riot of colours. I know some of their names: hocks, dahlias, roses. Sunflowers, sweet peas and viney clematis. Still, the novices remain inside, singing to their souls. Buzzing insects drift lazily through the warm air. The salt smell of the sea draws me onwards and, leaving the garden, I find myself on the forest path. The heat, though better beneath the shade of the trees, yet agitates me, and I pull at the loose, belted tunic in which the novices insist on dressing me in, imagining already the blissful relief of lying in the shallows.

I rest for a moment and then begin again, one crutch forward, then the next, battling for every 'step.' I think I remember the way and, when the path splits,

I follow the smell of the sea's breath, pulling myself through the forest and toward the arms of the ocean. I think I shall lie where the waves break on the sand until the moon rises, listening to the rhythm of the water change as the evening draws in, watching the play of light on the horizon, feeling the cool kiss of my discarded home.

After an eternity, I emerge from the forest path, and the bottom of my crutches sink into the powdery dryness of sand. I blink in the sudden glare. The shadowed shapes of the trees remain floating in my vision. But, when I pass a hand over my eyes, the shapes remain. I realize they are not the ghosts of the forest but, instead, many people gathered on the beach. At the centre of this group is a small, open wooden structure, hung with many flowers. Beneath this structure, stands Christian and a woman. The woman, too, is strung with garlands of flowers, and her mouth is open in a laugh.

Without knowing I do so, I swing myself forward a few paces, until I stand, unnoticed, on the outskirts of the group. I remember Bethel's words, and I suddenly understand what I am witnessing. I turn hastily on my crutches, determined to get back to the sanctuary of the church as quickly as I can but, still clumsy on my surrogate legs, I fall, crashing to the sand in a tangle of limbs, tail, and pole.

As one, the assembled crowd turn towards me. Still struggling to gather my crutches and lever myself up, I hear a number of exclamations and a few bursts of laughter. But mostly they are silent, watching me writhing on the sand.

And then Christian is at my side, supporting me at the waist so that I can get my balance. I cling to him as though I am drowning in air and only he can pull me back to the deep.

A voice explodes, its owner striding towards us: "Christian! Get away from her!" It is Janka.

"She needs help…" Christian begins.

"She has a knife, man!"

In confusion, I look down at my empty hands…and see the coral knife, its hilt and the top of its shaft sticking in the belt of my tunic.

As swift as a sea snake, Christian jumps back from me. He grabs blindly behind him for the hand of his bride. Without turning to her, he orders her back to the village.

"Christian!" I sign. "It is not mine!" I pull the coral knife from my belt, meaning to throw it down, but before I can, Janka and one of his fellows are on me, trying to wrestle it from my hand.

Dimly, I hear Christian shouting at the assembled humans, ordering them off the beach, herding them into the forest.

Janka kicks my crutches out from under me, and I go down, hard, to the sand. His friend strikes at me and I lash out, catching the man across his ankle with the lethal blade of the coral knife that has appeared from nowhere in my belt. He howls, grabbing at his leg and rolling on the ground. Janka, ignoring his companion, puts a foot on my tail and bends, grabbing me by the hair before I can move away. I wave the knife in front of me defensively, making slashes at his torso and arm that do not connect.

Pulling my hair back harder, so that my scalp screams in agony, Janka kicks out brutally at my hand, breaking bones in my fingers and sending the knife flying.

"Janka!" It is Christian's voice, fast approaching. "Stop!"

Janka, momentarily distracted, looks up and, in that tiny bubble of time, I grab one of the discarded crutches with my undamaged hand and smash it into his face. There is a nauseating crunch, and he screams, raising his hands to his nose and eyes, blood welling and falling between his fingers like red jewels. He bends double, retching up gore and bile, and I hit him again, catching him hard on the side of the head. This time he falls, face first, onto the beach. When he does, I hit him again, even harder, on the back of his skull. He stops moving and is silent.

The crutch is raised for another blow when Christian catches it on the downswing.

For a few heartbeats, I do not see Christian, just another generic human who I must defend myself against. I try to force the pole from his hands, fully intending to club him with it and leave him, too, bleeding in the sand…and then the lines and details of his face register within my brain. And I see the horror and disgust that overlay those beloved lines and details, and all the strength leaves me. Without taking his eyes off me, Christian lays a hand on Janka's back.

"Janka?" he says. Louder: "Janka!"

"You have killed him," he says to me, wonder in his voice.

He looks at me. The way you would look at a dangerous animal. The crutches are both in the sand now, and he kicks them away from me.

I do not mean to use them again, anyway.

"Leave here," he says to me. His voice is haggard. "I cannot protect you from what will happen next." He turns from me, and begins to stride up the beach, towards the forest. Before he does, he looks back, one last time.

"Janka and the others were right," he says. "I had always dreamed that we could seek out your specics, if the tales were true, and learn much, each from the other. But you are simply primitive humans, a backward evolutionary step. You are an abomination."

And then he leaves, and the forest closes over him like a healed wound.

I do not cry this time. The waves, in the gathering dusk, mouth their way higher up the beach, and I am there to meet them. I lie back and let them gather me up and bear me out on their silky current. I watch the purpling sky wheel and dip above me as, arms outstretched, I drift further and further from land, feeling the water cool and darken beneath me. I know that, soon, it will pull me under and without breath, I shall die. My body, over time, will melt into the living fabric of the ocean. I am content for this to be so. I have lived among the humans; I have smelt the perfume of spring flowers drizzled in warm rain; I have felt the warm press of blankets and heard wolves howling on the hillside; I have stroked the feathers of a caged bird and I have touched the breathing skin of a human who looked at me without fear.

Full night has fallen and the stars are a white-blue spangle turning in a cluster above me when I feel my body succumb to the water as exhaustion overtakes me in a thick torrent. My tail no longer undulates just below the surface, and my arms droop to my sides. I begin to sink. The stars waver and flicker as my head drops beneath the waves. I let it happen and am plummeting, stone like, the last of the air in my body gone, when suddenly I am borne aloft. I am rising back towards the surface on an unseen tide.

I realise that strong arms are pulling me upwards. The side of a head presses against mine. Breaking the surface, pulling in air in huge heaves, I see that it is Farner. He holds me up, bobbing beside me, having to hold his breath dry-side.

I forget my lost voice, and try to exclaim: "Farner!"

He looks at me, taking in everything. The bandages around my neck that trail behind me like the poison tails of a jellyfish. The cuts on my face and my smashed hand. The look in my eyes. He can't know it all, but he knows me, and that is enough.

"Hush, now," he soothes. "I'm going to take you home." His gills are straining in the dry air, and I know he will have to dive beneath the water's surface soon.

He places my arm around his neck, and when he dips beneath the waves, I hold tight to him, supported on the silver muscles of his back as he moves through the sea. I think of the homecoming I will receive. I imagine the half-life I will lead, somewhere between the land and the sea.

But mostly, I think of the red flower Farner brought me from the shore, so long ago. And, thinking of that flower, given at such a cost, and riding the surge of the tide with the night sky unspooling high above me, I close my eyes. It is like neither swimming in my old existence or walking in the life I thought I wanted. I am flying, cresting the waves and soaring above them, as insubstantial as foam.

Far below me, I hear Farner calling my name – "Severance! Severance! You must wake up!" – but I think I would rather sleep, and dream.

ABOUT THE AUTHOR

M A Smith lives in Gloucestershire, UK. Her fiction has appeared in publications including Gathering Storm Magazine, Haunted Waters Press' 'From the Depths' Anthology and Dark Moon Digest. Find out more at www.masmithwriting.com.

Printed in Great Britain
by Amazon